GERTIE THE GOLDFISH

and the Christmas Surprise

By
Naomi Judd

Illustrations by
Tom Bancroft & Rob Corley

A Division of Thomas Nelson Publishers
Since 1798

For other life-changing resources, visit us at
www.thomasnelson.com

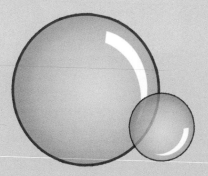

Jacket & Interior Design: Troy Birdsong • Funnypages Productions
Colorist: Jon Conkling • Funnypages Productions

Published in Nashville, Tennessee, by Tommy Nelson®,
a Division of Thomas Nelson, Inc.

ISBN 1-4003-0780-5

Scripture quoted from The Holy Bible, King James Version.

Tommy Nelson® books may be purchased in bulk for
educational, business, fundraising, or sales promotion
use. For information, please e-mail SpecialMarkets@ThomasNelson.com.

Printed in the United States of America
05 06 07 08 PHX 5 4 3 2 1

Dear Parent,

Nothing is more important than the time you spend with your child. And nothing will ever replace a good book in helping to shape a child's imagination and imprint positive messages. Reading to children shows them that they matter and strengthens the bond between them and their family and community.

I'm a storyteller, and I care so much about children. To combine those two loves, I created Gertie—a goldfish looking out at the world from her fishbowl. As a celebrity, my life is, in a lot of ways, very similar to Gertie's. But I've learned that even though I am the one in the fishbowl, I also have a unique way to look out at the world. Through Gertie, my goal is to use this perspective to positively impact the lives of children everywhere, so that they, too, can learn to view the world around them with understanding and compassion.

Gertie is the name of my own pet goldfish. My family and I sense her watching our every move from her bowl perched on the kitchen counter. In this beautifully illustrated book, Gertie is given a voice, sharing important life lessons with Emily and Josh McKay as she watches over the family.

My hope is that Gertie will become a special part of your family too, sharing invaluable lessons with your children as they make their own place in this world.

This first book in the Gertie series is dedicated to my own book-loving grandkids, Elijah and Grace Judd.

Still in One Peace,

Naomi Judd

It's finally Christmas, and the toy store is bustling
With children laughing and squealing.
Every new toy that a kid could imagine
Is stacked from the floor to the ceiling!

One little boy, while test-driving a bike,
Bumps into the wall with a *BOOM*!
Suddenly a fishbowl falls from the top shelf,
Splashing water all over the room!

In all of the chaos, no one seems to notice
The goldfish that just lost her home.
Gertie the Goldfish has lived there for years,
And she's used to being alone.

Through the sea of people, a young girl and her brother
Make their way to Gertie's side.
They pick up the fish and place her in the fountain,
Knowing that will keep her alive.

Gertie soaks in the water, swims in a circle,
And thanks them with a flap of her fin.
Josh and Emily smile at their parents,
Hoping that they'll get the hint.

Mom and Dad laugh, because they both know
What the kids are trying to say:
A little goldfish would be the perfect gift
To receive on Christmas Day.

Later that night, the kids can't sleep
As they think about the bright-eyed fish.
Emily's eyes glisten and grow wide with hope
As she makes a quiet Christmas wish.

"I've never seen such a pretty fish," she whispers,
In the light of the white, winter moon.
"Oh please, oh please, somehow, some way,
Let that fish be ours really soon!"

The next morning, the kids climb on the school bus,
Still beaming from the day before.
"Hey, Bobby!" Josh begins with a smile.
"Guess what I saw yesterday at the store?!"

Josh tells his friends all about Gertie;
And soon, the whole bus is listening to him.
"She's shiny and yellow!" he exclaims with a smile.
"You won't believe how fast she can swim!"

Then a boy from the back of the bus yells out,
To Josh and Emily's surprise,
"Is that *all* you want for Christmas?" he teases.
"A stupid fish can't even run outside!"

The other kids tease, and Josh puts down his head;
His eyes fill up with tears.
"Don't listen to them, Josh. Don't listen to a word,"
Emily quietly says in his ear.

The kids on the bus quickly forget
About the story of Gertie the fish.
They soon start to talk about all of the things
That are on *their* Christmas lists.

There are dolls, bikes, and computer games—
Everything under the sun!
After a while, a little goldfish
Doesn't seem like that much fun.

The school day goes by so slowly
For Josh and Emily McKay;
Their hearts are still sad when they arrive home
At the end of the long, long day.

A few snow flurries begin to fall
As they walk up to their front door.
Usually they love to play in the snow,
But they're not in the mood anymore.

As they come in the door, they drop their books
In a sudden, newfound glee,
For just inside, a gift is waiting for them
Underneath the Christmas tree!

They can't hide their joy as they run to the gift,
Almost tripping over their dog, Tilly;
They drop to their knees, surprised, excited,
And simply just plain silly!

"Hi, kids!" says Mommy with two big hugs;
The kids look up with wide-open eyes.
"That's right! Dad and I decided to get you
An early Christmas surprise!"

Josh and Emily erupt into giggles
As they rip off the bright, red bow.
Inside is the most wonderful sight—
It's Gertie, swimming in her bowl!

"Gertie!" they squeal as they hug their mom,
Say thanks, and then squeal again.
Mom smiles as she leaves them to play
With their newest, most special friend.

When Christmas Day finally arrives,
Josh proclaims, "Gertie, merry Christmas to you!"
But he isn't prepared for the reply,
"Merry Christmas to you too!"

Josh and Emily can't believe it!
The kids are in complete shock!
"Let me explain," Gertie begins with a laugh,
"I know fish aren't supposed to talk."

"Remember in the store how you picked me?
Well, the truth is, I chose you too.
You saved me when I needed it most,
⠀⠀⠀⠀And now I've come here to help you!

⠀⠀"I don't have ears, but I can hear
⠀⠀⠀⠀Every thought that goes through your mind,
⠀⠀⠀⠀⠀When you're happy or lonely or just plain sad
⠀⠀⠀⠀Because someone has been unkind.

⠀⠀"I don't have legs, so I can't walk
⠀⠀⠀Or even leave this bowl,
⠀⠀⠀⠀But I have a heart so that we can talk
⠀⠀⠀In a language all our own!"

"I've heard you talk about that day on the bus
When other kids made you feel very small,
But I'm here to remind you that you are blessed;
You have nothing to want for at all!

"Your mommy and daddy have been here with you
Right from the very start.
And they have given you so much love
That it can't even fit in your heart!

"You have each other and a place to live
And food to eat every day.
You see, you really have the very best gifts
When you choose to look at life that way!"

Josh asks, "But what about what the other kids have,
Like expensive toys and fancy clothes?"
"It's not always easy," Gertie explains,
"But we should be thankful no matter how life goes."

Thinking a while, the kids smile at each other,
Realizing that life's not so bad.
"Gertie's right," Emily says, "and we need to thank God
For all we have and be glad!"

Later that day, the McKay family gathers
'Round the table as they do every night.
Outside the ground is covered with snow;
It's all such a beautiful sight!

"Merry Christmas!" they cheer as they eat a warm meal
Prepared with the greatest love.
The family is happy because all they could need
Is given from God above.

"And it came to pass in those days, that there went out a decree from Caesar Augustus, that all the world should be taxed. . . . And Joseph also went . . . unto the city of David, which is called Bethlehem . . . to be taxed with Mary his espoused wife, being great with child. And so it was, that, while they were there, the days were accomplished that she should be delivered. And she brought forth her firstborn son, and wrapped him in swaddling clothes, and laid him in a manger. . . ."

Luke 2:1, 4–7

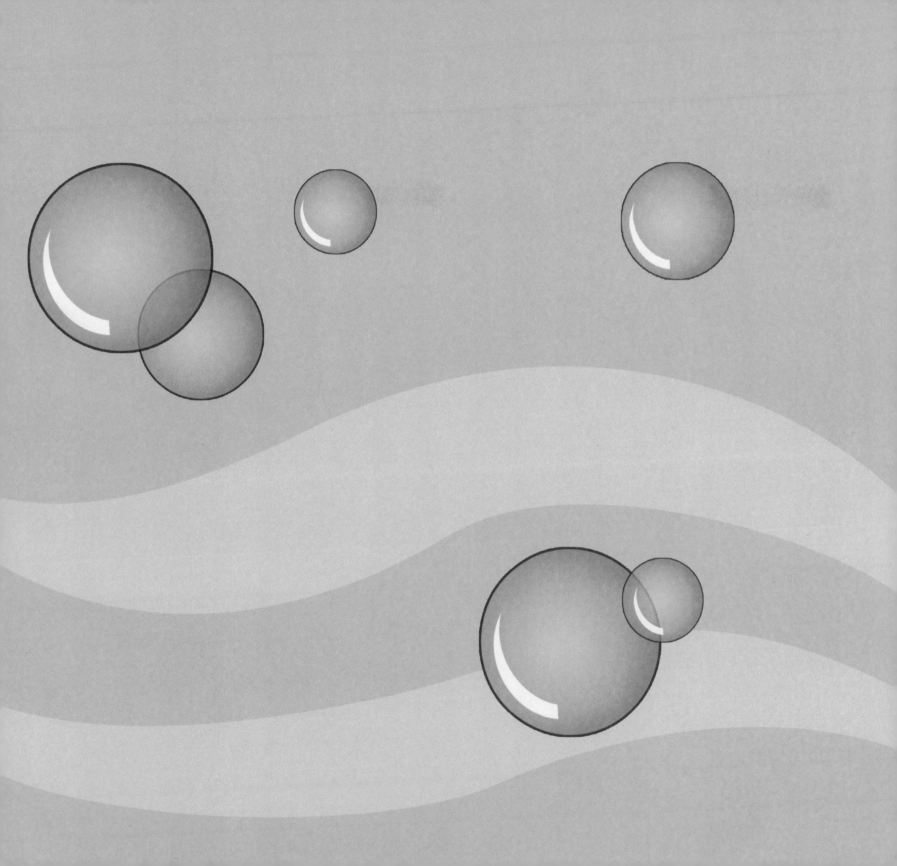

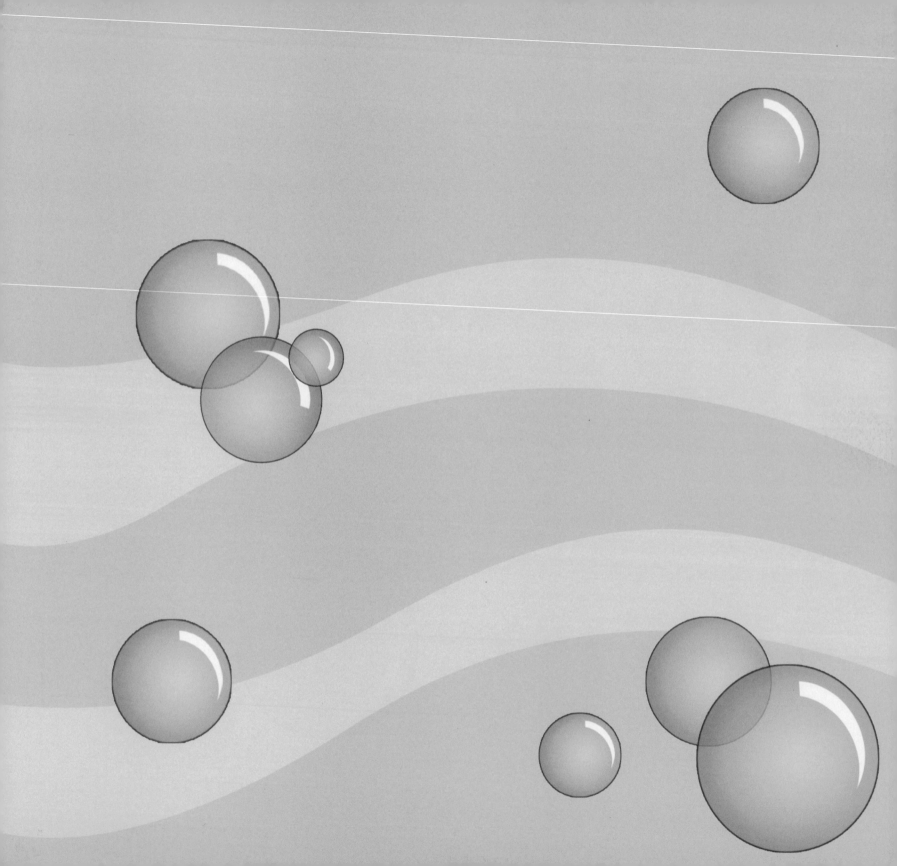